MY SON JOHN

BY
JIM AYLESWORTH

WOODCUTS
BY
DAVID FRAMPTON

HENRY HOLT AND COMPANY

NEW YORK

Yellow yellow sunup,
My son Ed.
Up he jumps
From out of bed.
On go pants
And wool shirt red.
Yellow yellow sunup,
My son Ed.

Rosy rosy robin,
My daughter Sue.
Eggs a-frying,
Down she flew.
Hair in braids
And wool dress blue.
Rosy rosy robin,
My daughter Sue.

Merry merry maple,
My son Jake.
Spreads sweet butter
On his pancake.
He'll eat his
And all Ma'll make.
Merry merry maple,
My son Jake.

Dusty dusty cobweb,
My daughter Ann.
Helps fill up
The tall milk can.
Cows in stalls
And pups round pans.
Dusty dusty cobweb,
My daughter Ann.

Chipper chipper woodpile,
My son Neil.
Lays his axe
To the grinding wheel.
Handle's oak
And head's of steel.
Chipper chipper woodpile,
My son Neil.

Bonny bonny bridle,
My daughter Rose.
Combs her mare
In old work clothes.
Hay in hair
And dirt on nose.
Bonny bonny bridle,
My daughter Rose.

Paper paper pencil,
My son Brad.
He is rarely
Ever bad.
He can spell
And he can add.
Paper paper pencil,
My son Brad.

Hi

Dilly dilly dingdong,
My daughter Lynn.
Rings the bell
To call folks in.
Hired hands
And all us kin.
Dilly dilly dingdong,
My daughter Lynn.

Jolly jolly june bug,
My son Joe.
Weeds the garden
Row by row.
Rusty gate
And ol' scarecrow.
Jolly jolly june bug,
My son Joe.

Clover clover ivy,
My daughter Pam.
Takes good care ♣
Of her pet lambs.
One's a ewe ♣
And one's a ram.
Clover clover ivy,
My daughter Pam.

Swirly swirly icing,
My son Pete
Chocolate cake's
His supper treat.
Creamy rich
And oh so sweet.
Swirly swirly icing,
My son Pete.

Fuzzy fuzzy pom-pom,
My daughter Fay.
Her three cats
Want her to play.
Two are black
And one is gray.
Fuzzy fuzzy pom-pom,
My daughter Fay.

Flicker flicker golden,
My son Rick.
He reads rhymes
By candlestick.
One great egg
And wall of brick.
Flicker flicker golden,
My son Rick.

Snowy snowy pillow,
My daughter Kate.
Up she goes,
It's getting late.
Stars are out
And clock's struck eight.
Snowy snowy pillow,
My daughter Kate.

Diddle diddle dumpling,
My son John.
Went to bed
With his trousers on.
One shoe off
And one shoe on.
Diddle diddle dumpling,
My son John.

For my sons, John and Daniel
—J. A.

For my son, David, and to my daughter, Sarah
—D. F.

Henry Holt and Company, Inc.
Publishers since 1866
115 West 18th Street
New York, New York 10011

Henry Holt is a registered
trademark of Henry Holt and Company, Inc.

Text copyright © 1994 by Jim Aylesworth
Illustrations copyright © 1994 by David Frampton
All rights reserved.
Published in Canada by Fitzhenry & Whiteside Ltd.,
195 Allstate Parkway, Markham, Ontario L3R 4T8.

Library of Congress Cataloging-in-Publication Data
Aylesworth, Jim.
My son John / Jim Aylesworth; woodcuts by David Frampton.
Summary: Depicts, in rhyming text and illustrations, the daily
chores and activities of a group of children on a large farm.
[1. Farm life—Fiction.   2. Stories in rhyme.]
I. Frampton, David, ill.   II. Title.
PZ8.3.M95My   1994   [E]—dc20   92-27192

ISBN 0-8050-1725-9 / First Edition—1994
Printed in the United States of America on acid-free paper. ∞
1   3   5   7   9   10   8   6   4   2